Prince Peter
and the Teddy Bear

for Amélie Giulia,
my first Grandchild

A Red Fox Book

Published by Random House Children's Books
20 Vauxhall Bridge Road, London SW1V 2SA

A division of Random House UK Ltd
London Melbourne Sydney Auckland
Johannesburg and agencies throughout the world

Copyright © 1997 by David McKee

1 3 5 7 9 10 8 6 4 2

First published in Great Britain by Andersen Press Ltd 1997

Red Fox edition 1999

Printed in Hong Kong

RANDOM HOUSE UK Limited Reg. No. 954009

ISBN 0 09 926728 4

Prince Peter
and the Teddy Bear

Prince Peter
and the Teddy Bear

David McKee

Red Fox

"It's your birthday in seven days, Prince Peter,"
said the King. "I expect you'd like a silver sword."

"No, Sir. Please, Sir, I'd like a teddy bear,"
said Prince Peter.
"A TEDDY BEAR?" said the King. "HUMPH!"

"It's your birthday in six days, Prince Peter," said the Queen the next day. "I'm sure you want a new crown."

"Please, Ma'am, I'd like a teddy bear," said Prince Peter.
"A TEDDY BEAR?" said the Queen. "HUH!"

"It's your birthday in five days, Prince Peter," said the King.
"I bet you'd like a big white horse."

"Please, Sir, I'd like a teddy bear," said Prince Peter.
"GRRRRR!" said the King.

"It's your birthday in four days, Prince Peter," said the
Queen. "I know you'd like a throne for your room."

"Please, Ma'am, I'd like a teddy bear," said Prince Peter.
"AAAAAH!" said the Queen.

"Only three days to your birthday, Prince Peter,"
said the King. "You can have a suit of armour."

"Please, Sir, I'd like a teddy bear," said Prince Peter.
"YEUIEEEE!" moaned the King.

"Two days to your birthday, Prince Peter," said the Queen.
"How about a nice new coach for processions?"

"Please, Ma'am, I'd like a teddy bear," said Prince Peter.
"OOOOOOH!" sighed the Queen.

"It's Prince Peter's birthday tomorrow," said the King.
"What can we give him?"
"Oh, for goodness sake, give him a teddy bear,"
said the Queen.

"Happy birthday, Prince Peter," said the King and Queen,
and they gave him a very heavy present.
"Thank you, Sir. Thank you, Ma'am," said Prince Peter.

"It's a teddy bear," said the Queen.
"A golden teddy bear," said the King.
"Thank you, Sir. Thank you, Ma'am," said Prince Peter.

"Goodnight, Sir. Goodnight, Ma'am," said Prince Peter
at bedtime. He took his present with him.

"Solid gold," he sighed. "How awful." And he put Teddy
on the chest of drawers.
He was woken by sobbing. Teddy was crying. "What's
wrong?" asked Prince Peter.

"I want to be cuddled," sniffed Teddy.
"But you're hard and cold!" said Prince Peter.
"I know," sobbed Teddy. "But I still want a cuddle.
Everyone needs a cuddle."

"Come on then," said Prince Peter and he cuddled Teddy.
"Very uncomfortable," he thought. But after a while he
murmured, "Strange, he's really rather cuddly." With that
he fell asleep.

In the morning, Teddy was cuddlier than ever.
"You aren't hard and cold at all now," smiled Prince Peter.
"That's because you cuddled me," said Teddy.

"Morning, Dad!" said Prince Peter when he went to
breakfast. Then, he gave the King a cuddle.
"Oh, ah! Morning, Peter," smiled the King.

"Good morning, Mum!" said Prince Peter and he gave
her a cuddle, too.
"Good morning, Peter," smiled the Queen. "How's Teddy?"

"Wonderful, thanks," said Prince Peter.
"I wonder what you'll want for Christmas?" said the King.

"Come on, Dad," said Prince Peter with a smile. "Eat your cornflakes before they go soggy."

Some bestselling Red Fox picture books

THE BIG ALFIE AND ANNIE ROSE STORYBOOK
by Shirley Hughes
OLD BEAR
by Jane Hissey
OI! GET OFF OUR TRAIN
by John Burningham
DON'T DO THAT!
by Tony Ross
NOT NOW, BERNARD
by David McKee
ALL JOIN IN
by Quentin Blake
THE WHALES' SONG
by Gary Blythe and Dyan Sheldon
JESUS' CHRISTMAS PARTY
by Nicholas Allan
THE PATCHWORK CAT
by Nicola Bayley and William Mayne
WILLY AND HUGH
by Anthony Browne
THE WINTER HEDGEHOG
by Ann and Reg Cartwright
A DARK, DARK TALE
by Ruth Brown
HARRY, THE DIRTY DOG
by Gene Zion and Margaret Bloy Graham
DR XARGLE'S BOOK OF EARTHLETS
by Jeanne Willis and Tony Ross
WHERE'S THE BABY?
by Pat Hutchins